D0129654

Brington and Whilton Pre-School

This book was presented to
Ben
We wish you all the best as you go to
School.
Love from Jenny, Jayne, Rose, Sally and
all at Pre-School

July 2005

OXFORD
UNIVERSITY PRESS

Great Clarendon Street, Oxford OX2 6DP

Oxford University Press is a department of the University of Oxford.
It furthers the University's objective of excellence in research, scholarship,
and education by publishing worldwide in

Oxford   New York

Auckland Cape Town   Dar es Salaam Hong Kong Karachi Kuala Lumpur Madrid
Melbourne Mexico City Nairobi New Delhi Shanghai Taipei Toronto

With offices in

Argentina Austria Brazil   Chile Czech Republic France Greece Guatemala Hungary Italy Japan
South Korea Poland Portugal Singapore Switzerland Thailand Turkey Ukraine Vietnam

Oxford is a registered trade mark of Oxford University Press
in the UK and in certain other countries

Text copyright © Jonathan Emmett 2003
Illustrations copyright © Adrian Reynolds 2003

The moral rights of the author and artist have been asserted

Database right Oxford University Press (maker)

First published 2003

All rights reserved. No part of this publication may be reproduced, stored in
a retrieval system, or transmitted, in any form or by any means, without the prior
permission in writing of Oxford University Press, or as expressly permitted by law,
or under terms agreed with the appropriate reprographics rights organization.
Enquiries concerning reproduction outside the scope of the above should be sent
to the Rights Department, Oxford University Press, at the address above

You must not circulate this book in any other binding or cover
and you must impose this same condition on any acquirer

British Library Cataloguing in Publication Data available

ISBN 0 19 279124 9 (hardback)
ISBN 0 19 272559 9 (paperback)

4 6 8 10 9 7 5 3

Typeset in Veljovic.

Colour reproductions by
Dot Gradations Ltd, UK

Printed in China

You can find out more about Jonathan Emmett's
books by visiting his website at
www.scribblestreet.co.uk

To Elizabeth J.E.

To David A.R.

Someone Bigger

Jonathan Emmett   Adrian Reynolds

OXFORD
UNIVERSITY PRESS

Sam and Dad had made a kite.
They'd made it large.
They'd made it light.

They went out on a windy day
to see if they could fly it.

'Can I hold it first? Can I?' said Sam.
'I'm old enough – I know I am!'
'No, you're too small!' his dad replied.
'THIS kite needs someone bigger.'

Then Dad let go
and launched the kite,

unwound

the string,

and held it tight,

while Sam stood by,

and watched,

and wished

that he was

someone bigger.

But the wind blew hard.
And the kite flew high.
And pulled Sam's dad INTO THE SKY.
And Sam went running after.

'Can I hold it now? Can I?' said Sam.
'I'm old enough – I know I am!'
'No, you're too small!'
his father cried.
'This kite needs
someone bigger.'

The kite flew up above the town,
where people tried to pull it down:

 a postman with a sack of mail,
a bank-robber, escaped from jail ...

... a policeman riding on a horse,
a bridegroom (and his bride – of course).

But ALL of them were pulled up too!
And Sam went running after.

'Can I hold it now?
Can I?' said Sam.
'I'm old enough –
I know I am!'
'No, you're too small!'
the people cried.
'This kite needs
someone bigger.'

And then, by some strange stroke of luck,
they flew right past a fire truck.

And when the firemen saw the kite,
they grabbed the string and held on tight.

But ALL of them were pulled up too!
And Sam went running after.

'Can I hold it now?
Can I?' said Sam.
'I'm old enough –
I know I am!'
'No, you're too small!'
the firemen cried.
'This kite needs
someone bigger.'

The kite flew on – it would not fall.
It pulled a rhino from its stall . . .

… and other creatures from the zoo –
a tiger and a kangaroo!

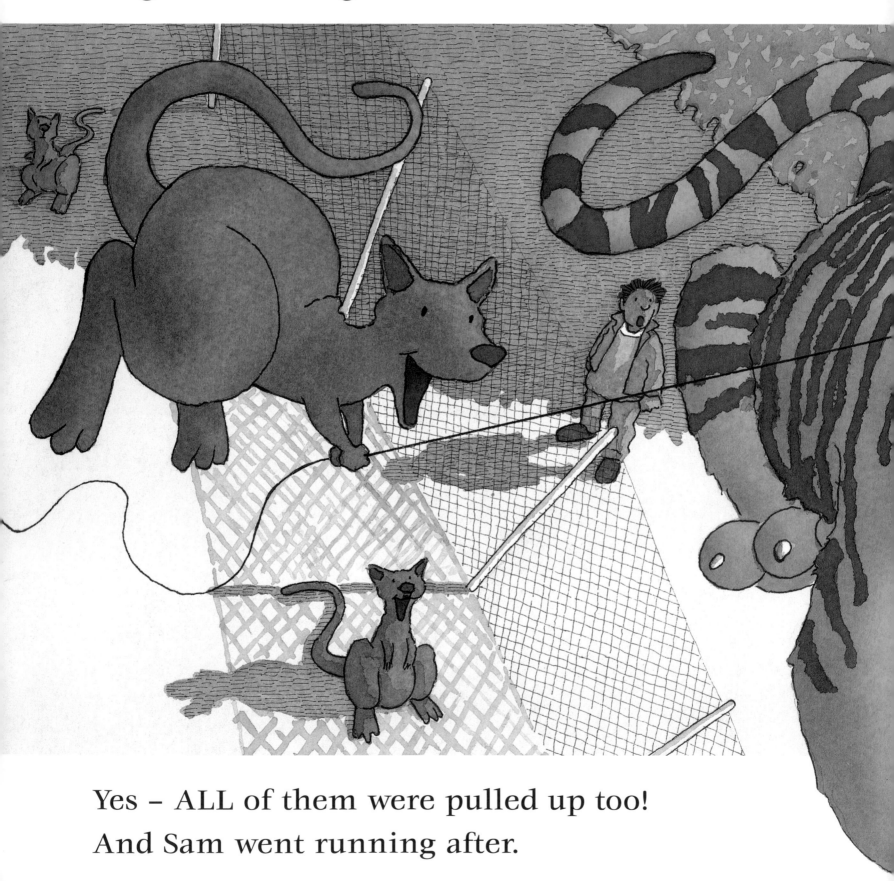

Yes – ALL of them were pulled up too!
And Sam went running after.

'Can I hold it now?
Can I?' said Sam.
'I'm old enough –
I know I am!'
'No, you're too small!'
the creatures cried.
'This kite needs
someone bigger.'

But then Sam caught the kite – at last!
He grabbed the string and held it fast.
And even though he wound and wound,
his feet stayed firmly on the ground!

And, one by one, they came back down,
everyone from zoo and town:

rhino, tiger, kangaroo,
firemen, bride (and bridegroom too),

postman, robber, policeman, horse,

and last of all, Sam's dad – of course!

'I'll hold it now,' said Sam, 'because
I'm old enough – I knew I was!
I'm not too small, and as you see,
this kite needs someone
JUST
LIKE
ME!'